OUT AT SECOND

THE #1
SPORTS SERIES
FOR KIDS

OUT AT SECOND

LITTLE, BROWN AND COMPANY
NEW YORK • BOSTON

Little, Brown and Company

Hachette Book Group
237 Park Avenue, New York, NY 10017
Visit our website at www.lb-kids.com

www.mattchristopher.com

Little, Brown and Company is a division of Hachette Book Group, Inc.
The Little, Brown name and logo are trademarks of Hachette Book Group, Inc.

First Edition: February 2011

Text written by Stephanie Peters

Library of Congress Cataloging-in-Publication Data

Christopher, Matt.
Out at second / Matt Christopher.—1st ed.
p. cm.—(Matt Christopher the #1 sports series for kids)
Summary: When a key player on the Grizzlies baseball team is hit on the head by a ball while practicing with his friends, they must decide whether to keep his injury a secret even after he starts behaving strangely.
ISBN 978-0-316-08481-9
[1. Baseball—Fiction.   2. Competition (Psychology)—Fiction.   3. Wounds and injuries—Fiction.   4. Conduct of life—Fiction.]   I. Title.
PZ7.C458Ou 2011
[Fic]—dc22
                                            2010008634

10 9 8 7 6 5 4 3 2 1

CWO

Printed in the United States of America

OUT AT SECOND

1

Zip! The baseball left the pitcher's hand and whizzed through the air toward home plate. The batter shifted slightly but didn't swing. The ball hit the pocket of Manny Griffin's mitt. He froze, waiting to hear the umpire's call.

"Ball!"

Rats, Manny thought. That was ball four. The batter tossed his bat aside and jogged down the base path to first.

Manny plucked the baseball from his mitt, threw it back to Abraham Healy on the

1

mound, and settled back into his squatting position.

C'mon, Abe, he thought. *We're just three outs away from the win. Don't give up now!*

It was the bottom of the sixth and the last inning of the game between the Grizzlies and the Wolverines. The Grizzlies were up by one run. But the Wolverines weren't beaten yet. There were no outs, and now they had a runner edging off of first base. Abe was looking nervous—and with good reason, for whichever team emerged victorious would advance to be in the championship game later in the week. The losing squad, on the other hand, would end its season then and there.

The next Wolverine batter stepped up to the plate. Before he got into the box, he knocked the dirt from his cleats. Three taps to the right foot, three to the left, and then one more to each.

Manny watched him closely. This Wolverine had been up a few times in the game. He'd tapped his cleats like this one of those times, just before he'd laid down a bunt. That bunt had taken Manny by surprise and landed the batter on base. Now the elaborate cleat-tapping routine had him wondering if the Wolverine was hoping to repeat that effort, or, at the very least, advance the runner to second with a sacrifice.

If so, I'll be ready for you! Manny thought. When the Wolverine took up his stance, Manny rose out of his crouch just a little bit. If the bunt came, he'd be set to spring into action.

Abe leaned forward, gloved hand on knee, and twirled the ball behind his back. Manny held up his mitt to give him a target. Abe straightened, reared back, and threw.

At that second, the Wolverine squared off toward the mound and slid his hands apart on the barrel of the bat.

I knew it! He's bunting! Manny thought. Adrenaline rushed through his veins. Manny was halfway up when the ball met the fat part of the bat; he was already lunging forward when it hit the ground. Because Manny was in motion, he reached the ball before either Abe or Luis, the first baseman, did.

"You got it, Manny!" Luis yelled. "Now send it to first! Quick!"

Manny scooped up the ball and glanced toward first. Second baseman Stu Fletcher was already there, covering the bag for Luis. Manny heaved the ball. The throw was right on the mark.

"Yer out!" the umpire called.

Some players might have stopped there, but not Stu. He pivoted toward second, ball cocked and ready to throw, clearly hoping to make a double play.

Manny looked at second base — and groaned. No one was covering the bag!

4

"Get to second, Sean!" Manny heard Stu yell.

Sean Wilson was a lanky beanpole of a kid and playing ball for the first time that season. He usually rode the pine, but that afternoon he was subbing for the regular Grizzlies shortstop, Jason Romano, who was out sick.

Manny held his breath. Would Sean get to the bag in time, or would he ruin their chance for a second out?

Luckily, Sean's long legs helped him cover the ground quickly. He held out his glove for the ball just as Stu unleashed a rocket of a throw. At that same moment, the runner stumbled in the base path!

Manny nearly let out a whoop. All Sean had to do was get the ball in his mitt, and they'd have two outs!

Sean almost bobbled the catch. Yet somehow, he controlled the ball, swept his glove down, and tagged the runner, who was sliding beneath him.

But did he make the tag in time, or had the runner beaten the throw? Everyone froze, waiting for the call.

"Out!" the umpire cried, jerking his thumb over his head.

"Woo-hoo! Way to go, Stu! Awesome catch, Sean!" Manny yelled.

Sean shot him a happy grin as he tossed the ball back to Abe. An instant later, however, that grin vanished.

"Time out!"

A thickset man carrying a clipboard hurried out of the Grizzlies dugout and headed right for Sean. It was Tug Flaherty, the Grizzlies coach, and he looked angry.

"That was *not* an awesome catch. It was lucky," he growled loud enough for Manny and the rest of the infield to hear. "And *you're* lucky that the batter isn't thumbing his nose at you from second or even third base!"

"Sorry, Coach," Sean mumbled.

Coach Flaherty went on as if he hadn't heard. "That should've been an easy catch. Know why it wasn't? Because you didn't look the ball all the way into your glove! If you can't even do that, you'll never be any kind of ballplayer but a lousy one!"

The shortstop hung his head. "Sorry, Coach," he said again.

Coach Flaherty slapped the clipboard against his thigh. "I don't need your apologies," he said. "I need your heads-up play. Think you can give me that so we can win this game?"

Sean nodded.

Manny bit his lip. He could see a deep red flush creeping up Sean's neck. Fortunately, the umpire called time-in then, sparing Sean any more humiliation.

7

Manny sank back into his catching stance. Even though Coach Flaherty hadn't been chewing him out, his insides were churning. *Sean made the out. So why couldn't you just leave him alone?*

He knew better than to hope that would ever happen. Coach Flaherty was a "screamer"; if he had a problem with your playing, he let you know it, loud and clear and in front of whoever happened to be near.

Manny wished he had the guts to ask Coach Flaherty to tone it down. But doing so would risk having the coach turn his anger on him. In the end, it was just easier to keep his mouth shut.

2

The double play seemed to have given Abe new energy. He threw four pitches to the next Wolverine batter. The first was a ball. The second zoomed past for a called strike. The batter clipped the third, sending it foul for strike two. He whiffed on the fourth pitch, a blazing fastball that socked into Manny's glove with a satisfying *pop* to make it strike three—and game over!

The Grizzlies infield surged toward Abe, laughing and cheering. The Wolverine batter, meanwhile, kicked at the dirt. Then his coach appeared at his side, put a consoling arm around his shoulders, and led him to their dugout.

Manny watched them with an envious eye. *Would Coach Flaherty have done that if it had been one of our batters? Probably not.*

He pulled off his catcher's mask and joined his teammates in the dugout.

"Nice pitching, Abe!" Kiyoshi Satou, the third baseman, was saying as Manny sat on the bench.

Abe grinned but pointed a finger at Manny. "He's the one we should be thanking," he said. "Seriously, Manny, you jumped on that bunt so fast I thought the batter told you what he was going to do!"

Manny leaned forward to loosen his leg guards. "He sort of did, I guess." He explained about the cleat taps.

Sean Wilson whistled in appreciation. "I can't believe you picked up on that."

Stu sat down next to Manny and gave him a friendly clap on the back. "That's our Manny—always using his keen powers of observation to get one step ahead of the other guys!"

Coach Flaherty approached the dugout then. He was smiling with satisfaction. "Good game, boys, good game," he said in his booming voice. "It was a close one, but you pulled it off. Now take a seat so I can tell you what you have to do to win us that championship title."

So much for the celebration, Manny thought as he moved over to make room on the bench.

The coach waited until they were quiet before speaking. "We'll be facing the Sharks on Wednesday. They're a tough team, but under normal circumstances I'd say we could beat them." He crossed his arms over his chest and frowned. "Unfortunately, we may be playing under circumstances that aren't normal — not for us, anyway."

The Grizzlies looked at one another, puzzled.

"I've just finished talking with Jason's father," the coach explained. "Jason's not here today because he has Lyme disease. You know what that is?"

"He's allergic to citrus fruits?" left fielder Gary Thompson asked.

Everyone broke up laughing.

Coach Flaherty remained stone-faced. "I doubt Jason would think that was funny," he said. "If it's not caught in time, Lyme disease can lead to terrible health issues like swelling of the joints, memory loss, and erratic mood changes."

The players sobered up at the thought of Jason experiencing any of those problems.

"Did they catch it in time with Jason?" center fielder Patrick McGwire asked.

"They did," the coach replied, "but only because he recognized one of the early symptoms, a red bull's-eye rash that surrounds a tiny tick bite. The good news is that he is on medication now, so he'll be fine. The bad news is he's not sure when he'll start feeling up to playing ball again. That means one of our subs may be starting at shortstop against the Sharks." He searched the Grizzlies until he found Sean Wilson. "Are you up for the job, Wilson?"

Manny saw Sean swallow hard. "I-I think so," he stuttered.

The coach grimaced. "You *think* so? Well, are you or aren't you? Because if you aren't, I can choose someone else!"

Sean straightened. "I am. You can count on me!"

His voice rang with confidence. But later, after the meeting had broken up and the players were gathering their gear, he looked anxious.

Manny noticed his discomfort. He nudged Stu. "He doesn't look too good, does he?" he whispered, jerking his chin toward Sean.

Stu glanced over at the sub. "He looks like he's going to be sick!" Stu stood up. "Come on. If we're going to win that championship, we've got to get him in tip-top shortstop shape!"

Stu walked over, planted himself in front of Sean, and said, "Tomorrow's Sunday, so there's no official practice. But can you meet me and Manny at Belford Park at two o'clock in the afternoon?"

Sean looked from Manny to Stu and back. "Why?"

Stu threw an arm around Manny's shoulders. "We're going to teach you everything we know about playing shortstop, that's why!"

Sean blinked. A small smile tugged at his lips. "Really? You'd do that for me?"

Stu snorted. "Dude, you're part of our team. The better you play, the better we do as a team. So we're doing it for *us* — all of us." He let go of Manny. "So, two o'clock? I'll bring some baseballs. Manny, you bring a bat, and we'll all bring our gloves."

Sean was grinning broadly now. "Two o'clock at Belford Park," he said. "I'll be there!"

3

Sean and Stu left soon after that. Manny was just shoving the last of his gear into his bag when he looked up to see his parents approaching.

"Manuel! You played a fine game!" his mother said excitedly. "Such a good throw to Stu for that out!" She clasped her hands in front of her as if to contain her happiness.

Manny looked down, embarrassed. He had inherited his mother's sleek black hair and deep brown eyes, but not her exuberant manner. He was quieter, more reserved; in that way, he was like his father.

"Nice game, son," Mr. Griffin said with a smile.

"Thanks," Manny said. "Did you keep scorecards?"

His father pulled out a notebook and opened it. On the pages were two elaborate tables, one for each team. Boxes on the tables represented innings, and a diagram of a baseball diamond for each inning was used to record what happened during each at bat.

"I haven't tallied the individual stats yet," Mr. Griffin said, pointing to the final columns. "Maybe we can do that together later?"

Manny nodded eagerly. He loved poring over the figures with his father. It was like reliving each moment of the game. And it didn't hurt to know who the best players on the opposing teams were, either!

Mrs. Griffin looked over her husband's

shoulder and made a puffing sound with her lips. "You and your charts and figures!" she said with a laugh. "Put them away and help your son with his equipment. I'm sure he wants to get home for his favorite dinner."

"Tacos?" Manny asked hopefully.

"Tacos," Mrs. Griffin confirmed.

Manny made a fist and pumped the air once. "Yes! Let's go!"

Half an hour later, Manny emerged from his bedroom, clean from a shower and ready to eat. He hurried to the kitchen, where he found his parents and his older brother, Matthew, waiting for him to join them. Or rather, his parents were waiting— Matthew had already started on his first taco.

"Sorry, bro," he said around a mouthful. "I was hungry!"

"No problem," Manny said as he slid

into his seat. "I would have done the same thing."

Mrs. Griffin had set all the ingredients—meat, cheese, shredded lettuce, sliced black olives, diced tomatoes, and crispy shells—in the middle of the table so they could all fix their own tacos. Manny took a shell, spooned the spicy meat into the bottom, and then layered lettuce and cheese on top. One big crunchy bite later, he was in heaven!

While the family ate, they caught up on one another's days. Afterward, Manny and Matthew cleaned the kitchen. Only when that was done did Manny and his father sit down together to look over the scorecards from the day's game. Mr. Griffin filled in the blank areas on the Wolverines card, leaving Manny to fill in those same squares for the Grizzlies.

When Manny tallied Sean Wilson's at-bat

efforts, he was surprised to discover that the substitute shortstop had three hits in five trips to the plate that game. One of those hits had gotten a Grizzly home to tie the game.

Those figures answered something Manny had been wondering about—namely, why Coach Flaherty had chosen Sean to start at shortstop over the other subs. After all, the coach hadn't seemed impressed by Sean's infield play. But maybe he *had* been impressed by Sean's hitting!

"Would have been nice if he'd said as much to Sean after the game," Manny muttered.

Mr. Griffin looked up from his sheet. "What's that?"

Manny sighed. "You know how Coach Flaherty likes to yell, right?"

"I'd have to be deaf not to know that," his father said drily.

"Well, I guess I just wish he'd yell good stuff to us sometimes, instead of always yelling about how we're doing this wrong or that wrong. You know?"

Mr. Griffin put down his pencil and adjusted his glasses. "Yes, I do know. In fact, I've been considering talking to him about his, er, coaching technique."

Manny widened his eyes in alarm. "No, don't do that!"

"Why not?"

Manny searched for an explanation that would make sense. "Yelling is just his way," he finally said. "And I don't think it bothers anyone else but me." An image of Sean with his head hanging low crossed Manny's mind, but he pushed it away. "I don't want anyone to think I can't take it."

Mr. Griffin regarded him for a long moment and then nodded. "Okay, I won't say anything. But if you change your mind," he added, "just say the word. And if you ever want to talk about it—or about anything else, for that matter—I'm here."

"I know. Thanks, Dad," Manny said, relieved.

4

When Manny went to bed that night, a light rain was falling. It was still misting when he woke up the next morning. It was ten o'clock, so he stood up, stretched, and went to the kitchen to find something for breakfast. On the table was a plate of bagels along with a note telling him that his parents had gone to do errands and that he should call Stu. He grabbed a sesame bagel and spread it with cream cheese before picking up the phone and dialing the Fletchers' number.

"About time," Stu groused good-naturedly.

"I called over an hour ago. Can you come to the field at eleven o'clock instead of two? Sean has to be somewhere this afternoon."

Manny peeked out the window. It had stopped raining, but the ground was dotted with puddles. "I can make it, but it's going to be a little wet, don't you think?" he said.

Stu laughed. "Look at it this way: the muddier the park, the fewer people who will be there to bug us. Right?"

"Can't argue with that logic," Manny agreed. "See you in an hour."

He polished off the rest of his bagel, drank some orange juice, and filled a water bottle to bring to the ball field. By the time he'd changed into his shorts and T-shirt, it was nearly eleven. He scribbled a note to his parents; grabbed his cell phone, his glove, and a bat; and set off for the park at a trot.

The mist had stopped and the sun was starting to peek through the clouds as

Manny hurried along the sidewalk. In ten minutes, he'd reached Belford Park. A combination sports field, playground, and amphitheater, the park had one of the town's three baseball diamonds. Sometimes, organized teams reserved the field, so it wasn't always available for pickup games or practice sessions. But as Stu had predicted, today the field was empty, thanks to the earlier rain.

Stu was already there. "Finally!" he said when he saw Manny. "Come on, let's play ball!"

"Shouldn't we wait for Sean?"

"What would you rather do," Stu countered, "sit around or hit around?"

In reply, Manny picked up his bat.

Stu trotted to the mound with a sack full of baseballs. He dumped the contents on the ground and selected one.

Manny stepped into the batter's box. "Think you can find the strike zone?" he teased.

Stu went through a quick windup and unleashed a pitch that screamed toward the plate at top speed. At that exact moment, Manny recalled two things: Stu had a rocket for an arm — and he, Manny, wasn't wearing a batting helmet!

With a shout of alarm, he leaped backward out of harm's way.

"Interesting technique!" Stu called from the mound.

"Very funny!" Manny growled. "Why didn't you tell me I'd forgotten to put on a helmet? Do you have one?"

Stu made a face. "You know my mom always makes me bring one. She's such a safety freak! This morning alone, she made me put on sunscreen and bug spray, take my vitamins, and use hand sanitizer before I left the house."

Manny grinned. He knew that Stu thought his mother was overprotective. When it came to Stu's health, she believed too much caution was better than too little!

"The helmet's over by the bench with my other stuff," Stu said. "You can get it if you want. Or," he added as Manny took a step in that direction, "you can show that you trust me and not wear it!"

Manny stopped and looked at his friend. Stu tossed a ball up and caught it. "Come on, Manny, you know how good my aim is!" he said with a grin.

Manny snorted and continued to the bench. "Yeah, I know your aim is good," he replied as he fitted the helmet in place. "But if it's all the same to you, I'd rather keep my skull in one piece."

When Manny was back in the box, Stu faced the plate, reared back, and threw another sizzler. He *did* have decent aim; the ball flew just below Manny's waist.

Manny swung. *Crack!* The barrel of the

bat met the ball cleanly, sending it soaring off into the outfield.

"Whoo-eee!" Stu whooped. "That pill is gone!"

Manny grinned but didn't cheer. He didn't want Stu to think he was bragging.

Stu hurled five more pitches. Manny hit four of them squarely. He knocked the last one straight up into the air. Instinctively, he darted forward to make the catch, only remembering when the ball stung his bare hand that he wasn't wearing his mitt.

"Yowch!" he cried, shaking his fingers to ease the pain.

"Careful! Your fingers are just as important as your head!" Stu warned. "We need all your parts in good working order if we're going to win against the Sharks!"

Manny laughed as he hustled to help Stu retrieve the balls from the field. "Hey, where do you think Sean is?"

"Here I am!" Sean called from the out-skirts of the field. He hurried toward them. "Sorry I'm late."

"No problem," Manny said. "We were just doing a little pitch-and-hit to warm up."

"Now that you're here," Stu said, "we'll switch to shortstop stuff."

"Okay," Sean said. "Just tell me what to do."

Manny took off the batting helmet, scratched his head, and looked at Stu. "I'm not sure, actually," he confessed. "Got any ideas, Stu?"

Stu started juggling the three baseballs he was holding. "I'm full of ideas and all of them are good!" he quipped, his eyes following the path of each ball in turn. After a moment, he let them fall to the ground. "Sean, you go to shortstop. I'll go to second. Manny, you hit us some grounders and fungoes, and I'll talk Sean through different fielding situations as they come. Sound good?"

Sean looked worried. "That sounds good except for one thing," he said. "I didn't bring any fungoes for us to hit. Did you guys?"

Manny and Stu exchanged dismayed looks. *Does Sean really not know what a fungo is?* Manny thought.

All at once, Sean started laughing. "Man, you must really think I'm a dunce! I may not have played on a team before, but sheesh! Even *I* know what a fungo is!" To demonstrate his knowledge, he picked up a bat and a ball, tossed the ball into the air, and hit a pop fly. "Okay?"

Manny smiled. "Better than okay!"

"Let's go!" Stu agreed.

5

Stu and Sean grabbed their gloves and headed for the infield, while Manny took the bat and moved toward the plate.

He started off with an easy grounder toward shortstop. Sean darted forward, scooped the ball in his glove, and covered it with his bare hand.

"Pretend there's a runner!" Stu called as he raced toward first base. "Throw it here for the out!"

Sean tried, but he made the rookie mistake of releasing the ball while he was coming out of his pivot. Not surprisingly, the ball soared far off its mark.

"Whoops! Sorry, Stu!" Sean shouted.

"No sweat!" Stu called over his shoulder as he chased the ball into the dugout. "But next time, plant your feet and square off to me before you throw!" He tossed the ball back to Manny, and both infielders returned to their positions.

This time, Manny hit a fungo just to the right of the pitcher's mound. Stu moved in for the catch and then turned to look for Sean. When he saw Sean still standing in his original spot, he shook his head.

"Okay, if you only learn one thing this afternoon, it's this: When I move to the ball or to cover first, you have to cover second. If you don't, the runner from first has a free ticket to the bag. Of course, if you field the ball, then I'll be on second for the throw. Right?"

Sean nodded his understanding, and they returned to their positions.

Manny tapped a grounder that was supposed to roll midway between second and first. Instead, it headed much closer to first. He was about to call out his apologies, sure that the ball was out of play. But Stu surprised him by dashing forward, snaring the ball from the ground, and pivoting for a throw to second.

Sean had learned his lesson and stood on the bag, waiting with his glove stretched out in front of him. The throw never came, however.

"Hang on!" Stu said. "Sean, don't reach for the ball until you know where it's going."

Sean didn't seem to understand, so Stu came to his side to explain further. "If you stretch before the ball is thrown, you narrow down the area you can cover. Watch."

He reached out with his glove as far as he could go and then moved his arm to the right. "This position would be perfect if I knew for sure that the ball was going to hit my glove dead-on. But what if it's thrown off to the left? Now I have to move way over here." He swept his arm in an arc to his left.

Sean's face brightened. "I get it," he said. "If I hold my glove closer to my body, I can move it to meet the ball directly instead of adjusting after the throw. Is that right?"

"Exactly!" Stu said.

While Stu was explaining the catching principles to Sean, Manny stood to one side, nodding. He felt like a third wheel on a bicycle. He knew a lot about the game. But he was pretty clueless about everything Stu was saying!

When he said as much to the guys, Stu laughed. "I'll bet you know more than you think you do," he said. "You just aren't getting a chance to explain it because I'm doing all the talking!"

Manny and Sean laughed, too. "Guess we'll never get the benefit of my vast knowledge then," Manny teased, "since you never shut up!"

Stu continued to do most of the talking as they practiced. Sean soaked up the information like a sponge. Before long, he was making good catches and throws every time and the right decisions on when to move to the bag and when to field the ball.

"How strong is your arm?" Manny asked when they took a water break.

"It's strong," Sean replied confidently. "In fact, I'd hoped I'd get to pitch in one of our games. Guess not, though."

Manny shook his head. "It would have been tough putting you in the pitching rotation since the team already has Howie, Abe, and Domingo."

"But that doesn't mean you can't show us your stuff," Stu cut in. He picked up a ball and tossed it to Sean. "Go on, get on the mound so we can see what you've got! I'll hit and, Manny, you can catch."

Manny hesitated. "I don't know, Stu. I didn't bring any of my catcher's gear."

"I can try pitching without you catching," Sean offered.

Stu shook his head. "You need his glove for a target. Come on, Manny. It's just a few lousy pitches."

Manny knew that even one lousy pitch could still cause him some pain, but he gave in. "Okay, fine," he said. "Be careful, though, Sean."

Sean nodded reassuringly and then headed to the mound. When he was out of earshot, Manny turned to Stu, glowering. "If I take a fastball in the —"

"You won't," Stu interrupted, "because I'll

knock every one of his pitches out of the park." He used his bat to prod Manny to his spot behind the plate.

Sean took a few practice pitches to warm up. To Manny's relief, each throw hit his mitt's pocket without him having to move very much.

"I'm ready if you are," Manny told Stu. He spotted the batting helmet by the bench. "But I see you're not. Your helmet's over there."

Stu rolled his eyes. "Who are you, my mother?" Then he stepped into the batter's box. "Bring the heat!" he called to Sean.

"Okay," Sean replied, "but remember: You asked for it!"

Stu hefted the bat over his shoulder. Manny crouched down. Sean reared back to throw. Manny widened his glove to give him a bigger target—and then gave a yelp as a mosquito bit him in the back of his neck!

Stu glanced back at him. "What th—?" he started to say. He never finished.

Sean unleashed a bullet pitch that was high and inside. *Thock!* The ball struck Stu right in the head! He staggered sideways. Then he dropped like a ton of bricks at Manny's feet.

6

Manny's blood turned to ice water. For one agonizing moment, he couldn't move or speak, just stare down at his friend's unmoving body.

Sean sprinted up beside him. "Is he okay? He's got to be okay! I didn't know he wasn't looking! I'm sorry, I'm sorry, I'm sorry!" he babbled, his voice choked with fear.

That broke the spell that held Manny. "Quiet!" he said sharply. Sean's mouth snapped shut. "Hey, Stu, can you hear me?"

There was only a faint sigh that could

have been Stu or the wind in the trees. Then Stu groaned and pushed himself up.

"Take it slow!" Manny said anxiously. "Maybe you should just lie still."

But Stu had already rolled over to a sitting position. He blinked rapidly but didn't look at Manny or Sean. He didn't say anything to them, either. In fact, it seemed as though he didn't even know they were there.

Then, finally, his dazed expression started to clear. He raised a shaky hand to his head.

"Oh, man," he mumbled as his fingers brushed the sore spot. "That's going to leave a lump." He looked up at Manny with a wan smile. "Did you get the number of the truck that hit me?"

Until that moment, Manny hadn't realized he was holding his breath. Now hearing his friend make a joke, he let it out in a long, relieved whoosh. Together, he and Sean helped Stu to his feet and walked him to the bleachers.

"Where's my hat?" Stu asked as he sat down. Manny saw it lying in the dirt by the backstop. The ball had knocked it clean off his head!

"I'll get it," Sean said. He seemed eager to be away from Stu—and Manny couldn't blame him. He himself felt guilty for not convincing Stu to wear his helmet. How much worse would it have felt to have caused his injury?

Sean returned with the baseball cap. Stu took it but didn't put it on. He just sat there looking at it.

"Guess we should call it a day, huh?" Manny finally said.

Sean nodded and stood up. So did Stu, but he'd barely gotten his feet under him when he lost his balance and listed to one side. He clutched Manny's arm to steady himself.

"Whoa!" he said shakily. "Who moved the ground?"

Fear pricked at Manny again. He helped Stu sit down and then grabbed his cell phone and dialed the Fletchers' home phone number. After four rings, however, the call went to voice mail.

"This is the Fletcher residence," the recorded message said pleasantly. "No one is home right now. Please leave a—"

With a grunt of frustration, Manny hung up.

"Stu," he said, "what's your mom's cell phone number?"

Stu rubbed his eyes with his fingertips, blinked a few times, and then stared at Manny. "Huh? Why do you want my mom's cell number?"

"So I can tell her what happened!" Manny said, coming to sit beside him.

He didn't think Stu's face could get any paler, but it did.

"Manny, promise me you won't say anything to her! She caught me riding my skateboard without my helmet last week and hit the roof! She said she'd ground me for *weeks* if she found out I wasn't using safety gear—and that includes my batting helmet." He put his head in his hands. "If I get grounded, I won't be able to play baseball. You know the Grizzlies need me if we're going to win. And think of how angry Coach Flaherty would be if he found out why I couldn't play."

Manny's stomach twisted into a tight knot at the thought of the coach's anger. And Stu was probably right: The Grizzlies did need him. Manny had filled out enough scorecards to know that Stu was the best second base-man in the league and a consistently strong hitter as well. With Jason out sick, the Grizzlies were already down one starter. How would they fare if they lost Stu, too?

Then Manny eyed Stu's head. He was certain he could see a lump starting to swell where the ball had hit him. "Don't you think your mom is going to find out anyway, when she sees that goose egg?"

Stu touched the spot and grimaced. "So I'll just make sure she doesn't see it."

Using his fingers, he combed his sweaty hair forward until it nearly touched his eyebrows. Then he put his cap on.

"There," he said, "how's it look?"

"*It* looks fine," Manny said. "But *you* don't!" It was true. Stu's face was still pale, and his hands had been shaking when he put on the hat. "Please let me call your mom or dad!"

"No!" Stu practically shouted. When Manny pulled back, he lightened his tone. "Being in the championship game is really important to me. You know that. Promise me you won't tell!"

Sean cleared his throat. He'd been silent up until then, but now he put in his two cents. "I didn't throw the ball that hard, Manny."

Manny bit his lip and looked from one boy to the other. Both were regarding him with expressions that were half anxious, half hopeful.

"Okay," he said at last. "I won't say anything, but on one condition. You have to *promise* to wear a helmet from now on."

Relief crossed his friends' faces. "You got a deal." Stu stuck out his hand.

Manny shook it and then used it to pull Stu to his feet. This time, Stu didn't lose his balance.

"Need any help getting home?" Sean asked.

Manny replied that they'd be fine. He hoped he was right.

Sean lived in the opposite direction and was soon out of sight. Manny and Stu walked slowly toward their neighborhood. Every so often, Manny cast a sidelong glance at his friend. He was sure he was being sneaky about it—until Stu caught him.

"Cut that out, will you?" Stu grumbled. "I'm *fine!*" Then, as if to prove his point, he turned to Manny with a wide smile. "At least, I'll be fine once this headache I've got goes away!"

Manny smiled tentatively. "Does it hurt a lot?" he asked.

"Know those cartoons where the anvil falls on the cat's head?" Stu said. "Well, picture an anvil the size of Texas hitting my head. That's what it feels like!"

46

"Ouch."

"Yeah, ouch," Stu agreed. "But it's just a headache. It'll be gone by tomorrow, I bet."

"So long as you're okay…"

" 'Course I'm okay," Stu said. "If I weren't, don't you think I'd know it?"

7

Manny and Stu reached the Fletchers' house a little while later. Manny gave Stu his bag of baseballs and his glove.

"See you at school," Stu said. "And thanks." Then he disappeared inside and Manny went home.

There, he found his mother high on a ladder cleaning the gutters. As he approached, she yanked out a fistful of acorns and threw them to the ground. Unfortunately, Manny was standing beneath her when she did so.

"Ow!" he cried as acorns rained down on him.

"Oooh, so sorry!" his mother cried. "I didn't see you! Are you hurt?"

"Nah, I'm fine." Manny rubbed his head where he'd been hit. As he did, he thought of Stu. *If a few little acorns can make my scalp sting like this, how bad must it have felt when that baseball hit him?*

Then he shrugged. *Stu said he was fine,* he reminded himself.

At his mother's request, Manny spent the rest of the afternoon helping with the gutters and other outdoor projects. By dinnertime, both of them were starving.

Fortunately, Mr. Griffin had started supper. When they came into the kitchen, he lifted the lid off a big pot to peek inside. A cloud of steam billowed around his face. "Homemade clam chowder," he announced, turning to greet them.

Manny and his mother took one look at him and burst out laughing. The steam from the chowder had fogged Mr. Griffin's glasses. He laughed, too, and then removed the glasses to polish them, blinking rapidly as he did so.

Manny grinned. His father always wore the funniest expression when he didn't have his glasses on—like he was surprised to find that the world had suddenly gone out of focus.

It's the same look Stu had after he got hit. The thought came out of nowhere, and he frowned.

"What's wrong, Manuel?" his mother asked.

"Huh? Oh, nothing." Manny shook his head to clear it and hurried upstairs to change.

After dinner, the family watched a time-travel mystery movie together. It was a great film, with tons of plot twists and surprises, but very long. When it ended, he was more than ready to go to bed.

He awoke the next morning to see the sun shining through a crack in his window shade. He stretched and got up to get ready for school. His father offered to drive him in that day, and Manny accepted. It was only after Mr. Griffin had dropped him off that he realized he should have called Stu to see if he wanted a ride, too.

Oh, well, he thought. *He'll just have to sit on the bus without me!*

Stu must have missed the bus, however, because he walked into homeroom late.

"Overslept," Stu muttered when the teacher asked why he was tardy. Halfway down the aisle to his desk, he stumbled. The class tittered, but Stu didn't seem to hear. He slumped into his seat and stared at his desktop for the rest of the period. When the bell rang, Manny saw him start as if he'd been woken up.

"Dude, are you okay?" he asked as they funneled into the hall with the rest of the class.

"I didn't sleep very well last night," Stu admitted. He punctuated the statement with a wide yawn.

Manny lowered his voice. "How's your head?"

Stu shrugged. "Aw, it's fine. I have a little bit of a headache, but, like I said, I didn't sleep well last night, so it's probably because I'm tired."

They parted in the hallway, Manny for science class and Stu for Spanish. Their schedules didn't intersect again until lunchtime. Manny almost walked right past Stu in the cafeteria because Stu had his head down in his hands.

"You don't look so hot," Manny said, sliding into the seat next to him. "Is your head—"

"My head is *fine!*" Stu said sharply. Then he groaned. "It's my stomach that's bugging me. I bet it's from the cafeteria food smell. What are they serving, anyway?"

Manny glanced at the next table. "Looks like grilled cheese sandwiches."

Stu grimaced. "Well, it smells like grilled *toe* cheese sandwiches. I'm going to see if I can use the bathroom."

With that, he shoved his lunch to one side, got up, and left.

Manny didn't see him again until that afternoon, on the bus. Stu usually talked a mile a minute on the ride home, but today he just sat and stared out the window. Manny stayed silent, too, only speaking to his friend to say good-bye when the bus dropped him off at his stop.

He's just not in the mood to chat today, he

thought as he watched Stu shuffle up the walkway and disappear into his house. *Nothing wrong with that.*

Yet deep down, a little worm of worry had started to wriggle in his gut.

8

Coach Flaherty had scheduled a practice for four o'clock that afternoon. The Fletchers' house was on Manny's way to the park, so as usual he stopped by to pick up Stu.

Mrs. Fletcher opened the door. "I'm afraid Stu won't be going to practice today," she said. "He's in bed."

"In bed?" Manny echoed.

A shadow of worry crossed her face. "I think he might be coming down with a virus or something. He didn't seem like himself when he got home from the park yesterday, and after school today he went straight to

55

bed! For all I know, he has a fever, but he won't let me feel his forehead to see if it's hot."

She sighed. "Maybe I'm making too much of it, though. He says it's nothing, he just wanted to lie down. How did he seem at school today?"

Manny searched for an answer. If he told Mrs. Fletcher that Stu had had a headache and felt nauseated at school, she'd insist on giving her son a thorough once-over. Then she'd be sure to discover the lump on his head and the truth would come out. And when Stu found out that Manny had been the one to tip her off, he'd be furious.

Then a solution came to him.

"You know, now that you ask, he did say he didn't sleep very well last night," he said truthfully. "Well, anyway, I'll tell the coach he's not coming. See you!"

He hurried away before Mrs. Fletcher

could probe any further. His mind was racing. *Are Stu's troubles somehow connected to the blow he'd gotten?* He could understand about the headache—*anyone* would have one after taking a pitch to the skull. But would a hit like that make a guy tired or sick to his stomach? He just didn't know.

He arrived at the ballpark a few minutes late to practice. Coach Flaherty was displeased with his tardiness, but looked even more disgruntled to hear that Stu was home in bed. "What's his problem?" he growled. "Aches? Fatigue? Huh. Sounds like what Jason has. His mother should have him checked for Lyme disease."

Manny nodded. He supposed the coach could be right, although he didn't remember Stu saying anything about having a rash. Besides, the way Mrs. Fletcher covered him in insect repellent made him think a tick wouldn't want to go near him!

The coach gathered the team together then. "I'd hoped we'd only be missing Jason today, but it seems Stu won't be joining us, either. Nothing we can do about that, of course, but there is a piece of good news. Jason is doing better than expected and will be back at shortstop tomorrow."

While the Grizzlies applauded, Manny glanced at Sean. He wasn't surprised to see disappointment on his face. His expression changed to surprise a moment later, however, when the coach announced that he was putting Sean at second base that day. "Taylor," he added, "you'll play Jason's position today."

Taylor Jones was the Grizzlies' usual second-base substitute. He looked equally surprised at the coach's decision to swap him over to shortstop. Manny might have been, too, if he hadn't remembered Sean's batting average from the previous game.

Manny figured the coach was hedging his bets. Taylor was a good kid and a decent infielder, but he was lousy at bat. If the coach had to have a sub in place for the game, he would naturally want someone who could hit as well as field. Sean was the right choice in that case.

At least, that's what Manny thought before practice began. Soon after, though, he wasn't as sure. Sean had been prepared to step into the shortstop slot, but it was obvious that he wasn't as confident about his responsibilities at second.

The coach had started off with a simple around-the-horn throwing drill to warm up the infield. Sean did fine with that, but when the coach moved on to more complicated situation drills, he looked lost.

Coach Flaherty didn't help matters. He bellowed out commands and corrections so fast that even Manny, who had more of a clue than Sean about how to play second base, had trouble following the instructions. After several frustrating minutes, Sean looked ready to drop his glove and walk away.

Manny didn't want to see that happen. He liked Sean and thought he showed promise as a ballplayer. He realized, too, that Stu had been right the day before: Manny knew more about what infielders were supposed to do than he thought he did. He also remembered what Stu had said to Sean about them being a team and how when one player improved, the team improved as a whole.

With that in mind, he screwed up his courage and approached the coach with a suggestion.

"Coach Flaherty, if you want, I could give Sean some pointers on playing second base," he said. "That way, he'll be ready for the game on Wednesday—you know, in case Stu isn't feeling better by then."

The coach considered the idea and then nodded. "Can't hurt. Might help. Find a spot off the field somewhere and go over the basics with him."

"Thanks, Manny," Sean said as they jogged to a vacant side of the field. "Maybe it's only me, but when the coach starts yelling like that, I just about can't take it!"

"It's not just you," Manny reassured him. "It makes me crazy, too!" He lowered his voice even though they were out of earshot. "Know why we don't have an assistant coach like a lot of the other teams do? He scared them all off with his bellowing!"

Sean stifled a laugh. "The way he barks, I sometimes think our team name should be Bulldogs instead of Grizzlies!"

"Yeah, and his growl is just as scary," Manny said, grinning. Then he saw the coach looking at them and added hurriedly, "Let's get to work!"

61

9

Manny crouched down and drew a base-ball diamond in the dirt. "As the second baseman, you own the right side of the infield," he said, indicating the area from second base to the foul line by first base. "If the ball is hit in here, you go for it. And after you field the ball, you send it to first."

Sean nodded but asked, "Should I throw the ball underhand to the first baseman to make it easier for him to catch?"

Manny thought about how Stu usually threw. "I'd throw hard. If you go too easy, he might have to come off the bag to reach the ball."

Sean nodded again.

"Of course, it's more important for your throws to be accurate and quick, not powerful," Manny continued. "Most times after you field the ball, you'll need to send it fast to either first or second for an out."

"The shortstop covers second for me when I'm not on the bag, right?"

"Right," Manny said. "And there are plenty of times when you *won't* be on the bag. That's because you'll be covering first when the first baseman moves in to field the ball. And you have to help out in other places, too. The outfielders have the strongest arms on the team, but if the ball is hit really deep, even they might not be able to get the ball where it needs to be in one throw. That's where you come in."

He pointed to the shallow infield on the diagram. "You head to the cutoff spot. The outfielder nabs the ball and throws to you. Then you have to know *exactly* where to throw to make the play. Of course, if the play is to home—to me or Ray Speroni, if he's catching that inning—then, yeah, you need a strong arm."

"Not a problem," Sean said. "I can throw pretty hard."

The memory of Stu crumpling to the dirt flashed through Manny's brain. Sean must have had the same thought, for he suddenly looked ill at ease. Their eyes met for a brief second before they both looked away.

"Yeah, um, so anyway..." Manny explained a few more basics to Sean, but his heart wasn't in it anymore. He was too busy thinking about Stu.

I'll stop by his house after practice, he

decided. *Just to be sure he's better. And if he's not...*

He shoved that thought away.

A few minutes later, Coach Flaherty called Manny and Sean back to the regular practice. He sent them to their positions and spent the next half hour running through drills with the infield while the outfield took batting practice.

Manny was pleased to see that Sean performed better than he had before they had talked. Sean shone when he was called on to bat, too, earning him a rare nod of approval from the coach.

Coach Flaherty gathered the team together soon after that.

"We have one more practice scheduled before the big game on Wednesday," he boomed. "To get us in the competitive spirit, I've arranged for that practice to be a scrimmage against the Dolphins. They'll meet us here at four o'clock. I'd like you all to show up at three thirty, though, so I can make changes to the roster in case either Jason or Stu is still out."

Ray Speroni raised his hand. "I'm going to Jason's house after this to see how he's doing," he said. "I'll tell him about the time change."

"I'll let Stu know, too, if you want," Manny put in.

The coach nodded his acceptance of both offers and then tapped his clipboard against his leg. "Hopefully, we'll be able to go with our original lineup. If we do have to start off with a sub, however"—he looked around for Sean—"Wilson, you'll be my first choice. I like what I saw from you out there today. Good work."

Manny and the rest of the Grizzlies looked

at Sean. Sean turned a deep red. *But at least this time*, Manny thought, *it's because he's flattered and not because he's being chewed out!*

Coach Flaherty set his clipboard aside and crossed his arms over his chest. "Now, about the championship game: You've heard this before, but it's worth saying again. It's not whether you win or lose but how you play the game. Right?"

The team responded with a chorus of "Right!"

"That being said," the coach continued, "I doubt any one of you will be happy if you go home with a defeat in your pocket. I *know* I won't be. In fact, I expect you all to bring your A game to the field so we can ship those Sharks out to sea!"

Practice ended with a resounding cheer, although Manny saw worried looks on a few of his teammates' faces. *Nothing like a little extra pressure from the coach to take the fun out of the competition,* he thought. With an inward sigh, he picked up his gear, shoved it into his bag, and took off for Stu's house.

10

Manny wondered if Stu would still be sleeping. But when he entered their neighborhood, he found him in his front yard, throwing a baseball against a pitchback.

"Hey, you're out of bed!" Manny called. "How are you feeling?"

Stu made a face. "Like an idiot for sleeping through practice! I can't believe my mom didn't wake me up when you stopped by."

Manny laughed. "So no more headache? No more stomach problems?"

Stu leaned over and picked up three

baseballs from the ground. "If I weren't okay, would I be able to do this?"

He tossed the balls one by one into the air over his head, the start of his usual juggling pattern. But unlike the day before, when he'd kept them going effortlessly, today something went wrong. The balls fell to his feet and rolled away.

"Guess my timing is a little off," Stu said. He tilted his head and squinted. "That, plus, the sun got in my eyes."

Manny glanced up. The sun was partially hidden behind a big cloud.

"So tell me," Stu said, bringing Manny's attention back to him, "was the coach totally cheesed off at me for missing practice?"

Manny dropped his gear, picked up a ball, and tossed it against the pitchback. "Aw, don't worry about him," he said, standing back to let Stu make the catch. "He was too busy ordering Sean around to think about you."

Stu paused in mid-throw. "Sean? Why was the coach yelling at him? I thought he was doing pretty well at shortstop after our coaching yesterday."

Manny explained that Jason was going to be back in the lineup the next day. "So Coach Flaherty put Taylor in at short and shifted Sean to second." He gave a little laugh and added, "Sean didn't have a clue about what to do in your position until I gave him a little bit of extra coaching. Now, thanks to my impressive knowledge"—he pretended to polish his fingernails on his lapel—"I think he'd make a pretty good replacement for you if he had to be."

Manny thought Stu would be pleased to hear about Sean's improvement; after all, he himself had said that when a teammate played better, the team as a whole played better.

But Stu just stared at the ground for a long minute. When he finally lifted his head, his eyes were blazing. "So you think Sean's better than me, huh? Some friend you are!"

Manny was taken aback by Stu's sudden anger. He held up his hands defensively. "Whoa, hold on! I never said that! I just said that he had improved, that's all."

"*And* that he should replace me," Stu said.

"That he *could* replace you," Manny corrected. "Not should. *Could*. But now he won't be doing that because, you know, you're fine and will be back at second tomorrow. Right?"

Stu eyed him with a suspicious expression. Then he blinked a few times and his face cleared. "Yeah, yeah, right. I'll be there."

"That reminds me," Manny said. "The

coach wants us on the field at three thirty so he can finalize the roster."

"Okay," Stu said. He tossed his ball from one hand to the other and then popped it high up into the air, following it with his eyes. But when he reached out to catch it, the ball grazed his fingertips and dropped to the ground. He kicked at it, muttering, "Stupid sun."

Manny didn't need to look up again to know the sky was thick with steel-gray clouds. He had felt the temperature change and couldn't see his shadow at all. He didn't point that out to Stu, though. Instead, he gathered up his gear and said he had to go. "See you at school tomorrow."

"Yeah, okay," Stu replied. "I have to go in anyway."

But when Manny looked back a moment later, he saw Stu still standing in the yard, staring at the baseball in his hand.

The worm of worry in Manny's stomach gave a sudden twist. He tried to ignore it, but it continued to gnaw at him through the rest of the day.

In fact, it didn't go away until the bus ride to school the next morning. He was in his usual seat and had just taken out his notebook of scorecards to look through when Stu boarded, slid in next to him, and started talking about the movie he'd seen the night before. He seemed so much like himself that Manny finally relaxed.

The movie Stu had seen turned out to be the same time-travel mystery that Manny and his family had watched earlier in the week. They talked about the film the rest of the way to school and were arguing over one of the more complicated plotlines in home-room when their teacher pointed out it was time to be quiet.

"I'll tell you why you're wrong at lunch,"

Stu whispered when the teacher's back was turned.

Manny whispered back, "And I'll tell you why you and your theory are out to lunch!"

But when the two boys met later in the cafeteria, Stu seemed to have forgotten all about their argument. In fact, he seemed to have forgotten all about the movie itself until Manny started outlining the plot to him.

"Oh, yeah, I guess I did see that movie," Stu said vaguely. "It must have been a while ago, though, because I don't really remember much of it."

Manny blinked. "But—but you watched it just last night!" No matter how much he tried to convince Stu of that fact, however, Stu refused to believe it.

So after a few minutes, Manny gave up. He gave up on eating, too. The worry worm in his gut made that impossible.

11

Manny didn't see Stu for the rest of the school day. After school, his mother picked him up and took him for a haircut, so he didn't see him on the bus ride home, either. And since he went straight from the barbershop to the baseball field, he didn't stop by Stu's house to get him.

If he had, then maybe the scene that played out later could have been avoided.

Manny arrived at the field just before three thirty. Several other Grizzlies were already there, including Jason Romano.

"How're you doing?" Manny asked the shortstop.

Jason chuckled. "A lot better than I was a few days ago, that's for sure! Who knew such a tiny little bug bite could make a guy feel so rotten?"

Coach Flaherty appeared then and pulled Manny aside. "Griffin, I heard Fletcher was back at school today."

Manny nodded.

"Then why isn't he here?"

That's when Manny realized that Stu was missing. "I don't know, Coach," he said. "I told him about practice starting early, just like I said I would."

The coach blew out a long breath. "Well, if he misses all of the warm-ups, he'll find himself warming up something else instead—the bench!" With that, he ordered the team to run three laps around the field.

As he jogged along, Manny kept an eye out for Stu. He knew he had told him about the time change—so where could he be? To his relief, he spotted him joining the run at the third lap. He slowed his pace to let Stu catch up.

"Good thing you made it!" he said. "The coach was—"

"Yeah, I made it, no thanks to you," Stu growled. "Why didn't you tell me we were supposed to be here at three thirty?"

"I did!" Manny protested. "Yesterday afternoon, when I stopped by! Remember?"

Stu squinted at him. "I guess I didn't hear you then," he said at last. "Sorry."

After the laps, the coach outlined the details of the scrimmage. "The Dolphins coach and I agreed that we'd play this as a three-two-count game. That means every batter comes to the plate with a count of three balls and two strikes. That way, our pitchers will get in some practice without tiring their arms, and the batters will get strikes to hit so the fielders can get some practice. And it will still be exciting. Got it?"

The players nodded as one so Coach Flaherty continued.

"Okay, now for the lineup. Domingo, you're at pitcher first with Ray starting off at catcher. Luis, you're at first. At second..."

He paused here and frowned at his clipboard. "Stu, you start off there. But Sean, be ready to go in for him."

He listed the rest of the roster in rapid fire: Jason at short, Kiyoshi at third, with Charlie, Patrick, and Gary in the outfield, and then reminded those who weren't starting that they'd get their turns, too. With that, he told everyone to find a spot on the field. "Easy throws at first, and then add in some grounders and pop-ups. Starters, I expect to see plenty of hustle out there."

The Dolphins showed up fifteen minutes later, and the Grizzlies left the field so they could warm up. When they were done, the scrimmage began.

The Grizzlies had the field first. Manny took a seat on the bench to watch the action. As an afterthought, he pulled his scorecard notebook out of his backpack and flipped to the game played earlier in the season between the Grizzlies and the Dolphins.

The same leadoff batter from that match was in the box now. Back then, he had struck out. Manny wondered how he'd fare today.

He got his answer right away. Domingo threw a pitch and *crack!* The Dolphin connected for a bouncing grounder toward third. Kiyoshi fielded it cleanly but didn't get the ball to Luis in time.

"Runner on first, no outs, play is to first or second!" Coach Flaherty reminded them. "You know what to watch for!"

Manny glanced at the runner. He was sidling off first. *A steal,* Manny thought. *That's what to watch for. And maybe a bunt to help him out?*

But the batter didn't bunt. When Domingo unleashed another fastball—*pow!*—the Dolphin laced a high-flying hit deep into center field. Patrick McGwire spun on his heel and ran back to make the catch. Meanwhile, the runner took off from first. Jason charged toward second to cover it so that Stu could race to the cutoff spot to get the throw from Patrick.

But Stu didn't run to the outfield. Instead, he made a move as if to cover first base— and then turned back to man second!

Patrick snared the ball for the out. But with no cutoff man to throw to, he didn't have a prayer of stopping the runner. He heaved the ball as hard as he could anyway.

Jason saw it coming and dashed forward

to pluck it from the grass. Then he relayed it to Domingo. The runner had touched third by then and looked eager to continue to home when his coach directed him back to the bag.

"Fletcher, what the heck was that?" Coach Flaherty bellowed.

"Sorry!" Stu said. He sounded bewildered. "I—I just...Sorry!"

Manny listened to his friend's reply with his mouth hanging open. He'd *never* known Stu to flub a play so badly. Never.

"You're lucky this is only a scrimmage," the coach said. "Now get your head in the game—or I'll put someone else in instead!"

12

The top of the first inning ended soon after Stu's error, but not before the Dolphins chalked up a pair of runs. Coach Flaherty rattled off the batting order, sending Kiyoshi to the plate to start them off. "Remember," he said, "you're going in with a three-two count. So unless the pitch is really awful, swing!"

Kiyoshi did swing. But he missed and was out.

Jason was up next. A lefty, he swung from his heels and sent the ball flying into shallow right field for a single. That brought up Gary Thompson.

"Lay one down," the coach muttered to him.

Gary did as he was told, squaring off to the mound for a tidy little bunt. The pitcher must have anticipated that move, however, because he jumped on the ball right away. He sent it to first in time to get Gary out.

Jason, meanwhile, was safe at second. But that's as far as he got. Stu, batting cleanup, stood like a tree at the side of the road when the pitch came. It whizzed by him at waist level and socked into the catcher's glove.

"Strike three, you're out!" the Dolphin coach cried.

Coach Flaherty scowled but didn't dispute the call. How could he? The Dolphin catcher had barely moved his mitt!

"Dude, why didn't you swing?" Manny heard Jason ask Stu in the dugout.

Stu just shrugged. "I thought it was a ball."

Jason shook his head in disgust. "Then you should have your eyes checked, man, because that pitch was as straight as an arrow!"

"Oh, yeah?" Stu retorted. "Well, I call 'em like I see 'em, and to me, that pitch looked lousy!"

Jason looked ready to argue further when Manny cut in. "Guys, it's just a scrimmage," he said. "It doesn't matter! Now come on, get to your positions before the coach has a fit!"

Jason and Stu glowered at each other. Then Jason pounded his fist into his glove and ran onto the field.

Stu reached down for his own mitt. When he stood up, he blinked a few times and then pressed his fingers to his eyes.

Manny looked at him with concern. "You okay?"

Stu dropped his hand. "For the ten-thousandth time, I'm *fine*. I just need to get focused on the game, that's all." With that, he slipped his glove onto his hand and hurried out to the second base position.

Stu seemed to settle down in the second inning. At least, he didn't make any more flagrant errors. He hit a sizzling grounder in the bottom of the third that went for a stand-up double.

After that inning ended, however, something happened.

"Okay, Grizzlies, I'm going to switch things up now," the coach announced. "Taylor, you head to shortstop. Manny, you're in for Ray. Howie, you take the mound. And Sean, go in for Stu at second. The rest of you will—"

"You can't do that!" Stu interrupted. His face was contorted with anger.

A shocked silence filled the dugout. For one long moment, Coach Flaherty seemed incapable of speech. Then he gritted his teeth and said, "I beg your pardon?"

"You can't replace me with *him*!" Stu jabbed a finger toward Sean.

The coach drew himself up to his full height. "In case you hadn't noticed, Mr. Fletcher, you're not the only one being replaced. Everyone is going to get a chance to play today. And I warn you now," he added, "one more outburst like that and Sean will see even more playing time, because I'll start him at second in the game tomorrow! Do I make myself clear?"

Stu clamped his mouth shut and nodded sullenly. He sat through the remaining innings in stony silence. When the scrimmage ended, he picked up his glove and stalked away right after the coach dismissed them.

Manny started after him, but then stopped. He'd never known Stu to be angry.

Even when they argued, Stu didn't let his temper get the best of him. In fact, until today, Manny would have said Stu didn't have a temper at all.

Something was wrong with Stu; he knew that now. But what?

A hit on the head couldn't cause him to act like this—could it?

He didn't know. But he decided it was time to find out.

13

When Manny got home from practice, he went straight to his computer and logged on to the Internet. He typed *head injury* in the search line. The computer returned a long list of sites to explore. He scanned the titles and found one marked "sports and head trauma." He clicked on it and was greeted with a prompt to view a short video clip. One tap later, he was watching a recent newscast from a local television channel.

"The sports scene suffered a tragic loss today with the sudden passing of boxer Sam Wheeler," a somber reporter announced.

"Doctors believe his death was caused by a blow to the head."

The scene switched from the news station studio to a doctor's office, where a second reporter was conducting an interview with a woman in a white lab coat.

"Doctor," the concerned reporter said, "we know that boxers receive hits to the head all the time. What made this one so deadly for Wheeler?"

"We believe that Wheeler may have already had a concussion from a knockout punch he'd taken a few weeks ago," the doctor replied.

"Why would that matter?" the reporter probed.

The doctor laced her fingers together. "Concussions are serious business—much more serious than many people know." She pulled out a model of a skull and opened it to reveal a plastic brain inside.

"Our brains are protected on the outside by our skulls and cushioned on the inside by spinal fluid. When a person hits something with his or her head or is hit on the head, the brain sloshes from one side of the skull to the other. It gets bruised, and like all bruises, it needs time to heal."

She sighed deeply. "If Wheeler had a concussion and was hit again — or more than once, as was likely, given his line of work — then any one of those blows could have damaged his brain so severely that it just couldn't endure any more trauma."

"But, doctor, what makes you think Sam Wheeler had a concussion in the first place?"

"As I said, he had recently been knocked out during a match. After the bout, he complained of headaches, dizziness, and fatigue," the doctor said. "These are all classic symptoms of a concussion, although they are not the only ones. Also, it should be noted that while Wheeler was knocked out, you don't have to lose consciousness to have a concussion."

"And had Wheeler chosen to seek help?" the reporter asked. "What could the medical profession have done for him?"

"The best cure for a concussion is time. With time, most symptoms usually go away within a few days or a week," the doctor said. "Until they do, however, anyone who has a concussion is at risk of greater health problems unless they take care of themselves properly."

Here, she looked straight into the camera. "I can't stress this enough: If you believe you have a concussion, you must protect yourself from another head injury. If you don't..."

Her voice trailed off and the scene cut

back to the newsroom and a photo of the boxer before he died. Then the video ended.

Manny stared at the screen without really seeing it. His mind was sifting through details of the last two days.

Stu had been so tired yesterday that he'd slept through practice. He'd said he'd had a headache, too. And dizziness — Stu had had that symptom, too.

Then Manny applied a mental brake. *I shouldn't jump to conclusions until I know a little more*, he thought. There was still time before dinner, so he returned to the computer's search engine and typed *symptoms of concussion*.

Once more, the computer offered a long list of sites. Manny clicked on the first one and scanned the article. The same symptoms the doctor had outlined were there, as were others, such as nausea and blurred vision. Manny recalled how Stu hadn't been able to juggle and had missed catching his own high throw. He'd left the lunchroom because he was feeling sick to his stomach.

Other words jumped out at him, too. Forgetfulness. Confusion. Anxiety. Irritability. With each new symptom, Manny's heart sank a little lower because everything he read pointed to one thing: Stu had a concussion.

His heart sank further still when he read about the number of concussions that occurred in youth sports. Football was at the top of the list, with an estimated seventy thousand head injuries reported in one year, but baseball was on there, too. One link even told about an old-time professional player named Ray Chapman who had died after being hit by a pitch. His death had eventually led to the introduction of the batting helmet, but those helmets were no guarantee that players would be safe.

Manny logged off soon after reading the article about Chapman. He drummed his fingers on his desk, thinking about what he'd learned.

He didn't want to ignore his findings. But he didn't want to break the promise he'd made to Stu to keep his mouth shut about the hit on the head. And what if he did tell, only to find out he was wrong and Stu was fine? Mrs. Fletcher would ground him, and Stu would never forgive him for making him miss the championship game!

But what if Stu wasn't fine, and then got hit in the head again in the game tomorrow? Manny shuddered.

Manny thought about his problem all through supper. It scratched at his brain while he was doing his homework, too. In bed that night, he tossed and turned, wondering what he should do.

The solution came to him at last. According

to the information he'd gleaned from the Web sites, the symptoms of a concussion went away over time, sometimes in as little as a few days.

Maybe, Manny thought, *Stu's symptoms will be gone by tomorrow. I'll just have to keep a close eye on him and see. Until I know for sure, I won't say a word.*

That settled, Manny finally fell asleep.

14

Manny put his plan into action the moment he got on the bus the next morning. He didn't dare ask Stu how he was feeling again for fear of getting the same "I'm fine" reply. So when Stu slid in next to him, he pretended to be looking for a particular page in his scorecard notebook. But really, he was studying Stu out of the corner of his eye.

He would have made a lousy spy, he soon discovered, for as usual, Stu caught him in the act.

"What? Do I have egg on my face or

something?" he asked, rubbing his chin with his fingers and grinning.

Manny smiled back. "No, no egg, although I think I see a little bit of toothpaste!"

"At least you know I brushed this morning," Stu countered.

"Or maybe last night, and then you didn't wash your face!"

They broke up laughing, Manny with relief as much as anything else. *He seems normal today,* he thought happily. *Maybe he's okay after all! Still, it wouldn't hurt to test him a little.*

"So, big game today," he ventured as they got off the bus at school. "Are you, um, planning to yell at Coach Flaherty again?"

Stu gave a rueful laugh. "No, I'd rather not be benched for the championships," he replied. He glanced at Manny. "Speaking of being benched, thanks again for not saying

anything to my mom about…you know."
He touched his head.

Manny couldn't believe it. Here he was, dying to ask Stu about his injury, and Stu was the one to bring it up!

"Yeah, about that," he said. "I was reading something online last night. It was about concussions."

"Yeah, so?"

Manny followed Stu off the bus. "So," he said, "I'm pretty sure you have one, and if you do, then it would be a really bad idea for you to play in the game today." The last part of his speech came out in a rush. It felt so good to get it off his chest that he let out a deep sigh of relief.

His relief didn't last long.

Stu stopped dead in his tracks. "Say what?"

Manny nervously shifted his backpack to

his other shoulder. "It's just that, according to some stuff I read, if you have a concussion and get hit in the head again, then you can be in big trouble. You know, health-wise and all."

Stu rounded on him. "So now you're a doctor? You can tell just by looking at me that I have a concussion?" He snorted with derision. "You think I don't know what's going on? You want Sean to take my place in the game today! Coaching him has become your little pet project, and you just have to see him succeed, don't you? For all I know, you guys planned for me to get hit in the head that day! Well, your plan didn't work, because I *will* be in the game today! And another thing"—he shoved his face so close to Manny's their noses nearly touched— "you say one word to the coach or my mom about my so-called concussion, and I will never, ever forgive you!"

He spun away and disappeared into the

crowd of students filing into the school. Manny, meanwhile, stood rooted to the spot, too stunned by Stu's outburst to move.

"Hey, Manny, come on or you'll be late!" Sean appeared at his side, took one look at him, and added, "Whoa, what is wrong with you?"

Manny shook his head. "I've got a big problem. And I'm not sure what I can do about it." He hesitated but realized that if he could tell anyone of his suspicions about Stu, it was Sean, because Sean had been there when it happened. So he told Sean everything.

"It's not your problem," Sean said when Manny was through. "It's ours. I'm the one who hit him. I'm the one he should be mad at, not you."

They walked into school together, both deep in thought. Then, just as they were about to part, Manny had an idea.

"You remember how Stu said that when we help one person on the team, we help the team as a whole?"

Sean nodded.

"Well, what if we apply that same principle now?" Manny said. "But instead of helping someone improve, we get the team to work together to protect Stu at the game today?"

"Okay," Sean agreed. "But how would we do that, exactly?"

"The first step is easy," Manny said. "We tell the guys about Stu's concussion. He only made me promise not to tell his mom or the coach, after all. And then, we figure out how to cover for Stu on the field. If we limit what he does, he'll have less chance of getting hurt."

Sean scratched his head. "It sounds complicated," he said doubtfully. "I mean, there's really no way of knowing what kinds of situations are going to come up in the game, is there?"

A slow smile spread across Manny's face. "True," he said. "But I have something that might help us." He reached into his backpack and pulled out his scorecard notebook. "These cards go back two seasons. That means we've got two years of info on every player on the Sharks, even if they were on a different team last year. I bet if we study their stats, we can make some pretty good guesses about what they might do when they're up at bat."

Sean whistled in appreciation. "It's a start!" Before they parted, they agreed to track down all the Grizzlies in school and to ask them to meet at the dugout as soon as they could after school.

Manny, meanwhile, spent the rest of the morning sneaking scorecards from his notebook and jotting down Shark player stats.

During his study period, he got permission to use a computer in the library. He organized the stats in a table and printed out several copies. He handed those copies out to his teammates in the hallways and during lunchtime. Then he wolfed down his sandwich and spent the rest of the time studying the information himself.

This may not work, he thought, *but if nothing else, we'll know those Sharks inside and out!*

15

The Grizzlies, minus Stu, were all gathered in the dugout by two forty-five that afternoon. They were all concerned about Stu and eager to help.

"Coach Flaherty will be here in less than an hour," Manny reminded them, "so let's see what we can come up with before then."

They huddled together and shared their ideas about what to do when particular Shark batters came to the plate and what to do during different defensive situations.

"One thing I'm worried about is what could happen if Stu misjudges a catch or a

105

hop on a grounder," Manny told them. "If that happens, he could take a ball to the head."

"I'll charge in on any grounders hit to my side of the field," Jason said.

"And I'll be more aggressive on those hit to shallow right infield," added Howie Timilty, who would be on the mound at the start of the game.

First baseman Luis Hawk said he could do that, too.

"And if I see you moving in," right out-fielder Charlie Eisenberg said to Luis, "then I'll rush in to cover first so Stu doesn't have to."

They continued outlining options for several more minutes. They were so intent on their discussion that they didn't hear Coach Flaherty approach until he spoke.

"Well, well, this is what I call initiative!"

he boomed. Then he frowned. "But where's Stu?"

"Here I am!" Stu jogged up. If he was surprised to see everyone else already there, he didn't show it. And if he was still angry at Manny, he didn't show that, either. In fact, he shot him an apologetic look as he took a seat on the bench.

The coach ran down the starting lineup. Stu smiled when his name was called. The other Grizzlies shot one another knowing glances and nods.

The Sharks showed up soon afterward. Slowly, the stands filled with fans. Manny saw his parents and a man who looked so much like Sean that he had to be a relative. He spotted Mrs. Fletcher, too.

The two teams took turns warming up. Then the umpire called for the game to begin.

The Grizzlies were up first. Third base-man Kiyoshi Satou selected a bat, swung it a few times, and stepped into the box. He let the first pitch go by for a ball. The second was high and was called a ball, too. But the third was dead-on. Kiyoshi swung and—*crack!*—sent the small white sphere sizzling between second and third. It might have gone for a single if the Sharks short-stop hadn't made a spectacular diving catch to pluck the ball from the air.

Kiyoshi wheeled around the bag and back to the dugout, disappointment etched on his face.

"You'll get 'em next time, K!" Stu said.

Jason moved from the on-deck circle to the batter's box. He clipped four foul balls before finally connecting squarely with one. The ball flew high in the air over second base. The center fielder raced in and caught it on a hop. He relayed it to first but was too late. Jason was safe.

Jason made it to second a few moments later, thanks to a sacrifice bunt from Gary Thompson. Two outs, man on second, and now Stu was up at the plate.

Manny was in the on-deck circle. He watched anxiously as the pitcher went into his windup. Stu was wearing a helmet, of course, but what if the pitch went wild and connected with his face?

He needn't have worried. The Sharks pitcher threw fast but true, just the kind of pitch Stu liked. Yet for some reason, Stu didn't swing.

"Strike one!" the umpire called.

Stu stepped out of the box and shot a perplexed look at the ump. He gave a quick shake of his head and then returned to his stance.

The pitcher threw again. This time, the ball dipped down just as it crossed the plate. It would have been a difficult one to hit, but Stu didn't even try.

"Strike two!"

This time, Stu looked frustrated by the call. And when the third pitch zipped by him and straight into the catcher's mitt for a third called strike—and the third out—he rounded on the official, mouth twisting in anger.

Manny quickly moved to intercept. "Tough break, Stu," he said, grabbing him by the arm and leading him to the dugout.

"Tough break nothing!" Stu fumed. "That umpire must be blind or something. I mean, you saw it, right?"

Manny spread his hands wide. "Saw what?"

"You *kidding* me? That ball was jumping all over the place! I swear, that pitcher has something in his hat that he's rubbing on the ball. You just watch and see if I'm not right!"

Manny guessed then that Stu was suffering from blurred or double vision. But what could he do? Stu didn't believe he had a concussion, so he wasn't likely to believe he was having trouble with his eyesight, either.

If only there was some way I could convince him, Manny thought as he struggled into his catcher's gear. *Maybe then he'd understand the danger he's in — and take himself out of the game!*

But until he thought of something, all he could do was try to protect his friend. With that in mind, he hustled to his position and readied himself for the action ahead.

16

On the mound for the Grizzlies was Howie Timilty. Manny had never been happier to see him there, for Howie was an ace. If he could throw a no-hitter for even one inning, then Stu would be safe.

That's just what Howie did in the bottom of the first. Three batters came to the plate; all three went back to the dugout without touching their bats to the ball.

Manny led off the top of the second for the Grizzlies. He let the first pitch go by because it looked wide to him. The umpire agreed and called it a ball. The second pitch, however, looked as big as a balloon. He swung with all his might. *Pow!* The ball sailed up, up, and up, before dropping to the ground between center and left field.

"Go! Go! Go!" Coach Flaherty yelled. And Manny did go — all the way to third! It was the first time in his career that he had hit a three-bagger. He could hear his mother cheering loudly from the stands, and knew that his father was proudly marking his at bat on a fresh scorecard.

Charlie strode to the plate to take his raps. He connected with the third pitch, but just barely. The ball dribbled up to the mound and into the pitcher's glove. The pitcher threw to first and Charlie was out.

Manny clapped as Luis stepped into the box. "Come on, send me home!" he called.

Luis complied with a sharp shot just to the left of first base. The ball was too far away for the second baseman to grab, and too shallow for the right fielder to get to quickly. When the dust settled, Manny was safe at home and Luis was on first!

But that one run was all the Grizzlies got that inning. Both Howie and Patrick struck out.

The teams switched sides. Manny's heart thumped in his chest when he saw who was up first for the Sharks. It wasn't just that he was that team's best hitter. It was where he tended to hit that had Manny's adrenaline flowing.

According to the scorecards, this Shark had lined more than one pitch right back at the mound. If the pitcher got his glove up in time, he had a chance to make the catch. But if he panicked and dodged, then that ball would keep going straight toward second base.

If Howie ducked and Stu backed up Howie as he was supposed to do, then Stu would be right in the line of fire. If he mis-timed his catch or couldn't see the ball properly...

Manny mentally crossed his fingers, hoping that Howie's reflexes would react fast enough for him to catch the ball if necessary.

But they didn't. When the Shark clob-bered the ball back at the mound, Howie jumped aside. Manny sucked in his breath — and then let it out again, because Jason had streaked across the field and backhanded the ball on a hop! He relayed it to Luis at first as quickly as he could, but the Shark was faster.

"Safe!" the umpire cried, slashing his arms out to either side.

Howie shook his head, clearly disgusted with himself.

"It's okay, Howie, just get the next one!" Manny called.

He took stock of the situation then. Runner on first. No outs. Sharks down by one. Manny gulped. If the Sharks coach had any clue as to what he was doing, he'd call for the runner at first to steal. Unless Howie could pick him off, stopping the runner from landing safely at second would mean a long bomb throw from the plate to second. From Manny to Stu.

Manny knew he could reach Stu. He'd done it plenty of times, in games and in practices. But he had no way of knowing whether Stu would make the catch. How could he "look the ball into his glove" if that ball was blurry or doubled in his eyes?

Manny decided that he just couldn't risk it. So when Howie threw his pitch and the runner on first took off, Manny bobbled the catch—on purpose.

"Throw to second, Griffin! Throw!" he heard Coach Flaherty yell.

Manny knew it wasn't a suggestion; it was an order. Normally, he would have followed that order. Not this time. This time, he did something he'd never done before.

He hesitated. Just for a moment. But that was plenty long enough for the runner to slide safely into base.

The Sharks bench and their fans erupted in cheers. Manny listened to them with just a hint of regret. His regret grew a bit more when he saw the disgusted look on Coach Flaherty's face. And when the Shark runner crossed home plate later that inning, it grew even more.

Then he saw Stu standing beside second base and knew he'd made the right choice not to throw out the runner. He heard his mother cheering. He glanced at the stands. There she was, standing and clapping. Next to her was Stu's mother. She was clapping, too, and smiling broadly at her son.

That's when Manny realized that while he'd made the right choice not to throw to Stu, he'd also made a grave mistake. So far, that mistake hadn't been a problem. But he knew that if something went wrong, it might prove to be very, very costly.

When this inning ends, he said to himself, *I'm going to do the right thing! I'm going to tell Mrs. Fletcher about Stu!*

17

The Grizzlies managed to end the inning without giving up another run. Manny shed his equipment as quickly as he could. He was batting fifth; if he hurried, he'd have plenty of time to explain everything to Stu's mother. He dropped his mitt and started for the stands.

"Where do you think you're going?" Coach Flaherty barked.

Manny froze. He'd been so intent on what he'd planned to say to Mrs. Fletcher that he'd forgotten that the coach expected his players to stay in the dugout when they weren't on the field.

"It looks bad when a player takes off during a teammate's turn at bat," he'd said more than once.

It turned out Coach Fletcher had another reason for wanting Manny to stay in the dugout, however. "What happened out there?" he demanded to know.

Manny tried to look contrite. "I'm sorry, Coach. I just missed it. It—it happens."

The coach put his hands on his hips "Yes, it does. But it's not the mishandled catch I'm talking about."

Manny swallowed hard. "Oh? Um, then what is it, sir?"

Coach Flaherty fixed him with a stern gaze. "If I didn't know any better, I'd say you held onto that ball instead of trying to get the runner out at second."

Out of the corner of his eye, Manny saw Stu swivel to stare at him.

Manny had worked hard all season long

to stay out of the hot seat with Coach Flaherty. Now he squared his shoulders and returned Coach Flaherty's gaze. "It was a — a judgment call, sir."

"A *judgment* call? There was no reason for you to use your judgment!" the coach cried. "I was telling you what to do! You would have to be deaf not to have heard me! Are you deaf, Griffin?"

"No, he's not, and neither am I," a new, calm voice said from behind Manny.

Manny wheeled around to find his father standing there. Coach Flaherty seemed too surprised by the intrusion into his dugout to speak.

Mr. Griffin laid a hand on Manny's shoulder. "My boy told you that he made a judgment call. Now I'm making one, too. I've held my tongue throughout the season, but now I'm going to tell you what I think about your coaching style!"

He was about to continue when *crack!* The sound of a solid hit echoed through the park. All three turned to see Jason drop his bat and race down the base path. Kiyoshi, who had earned a free ticket to first, was already halfway to second. He touched the bag and kept going. Jason sped on, too, not stopping until he reached second base. By then, Kiyoshi had made it all the way home!

The Grizzlies jumped and hollered with joy. But a second later, their whoops turned silent. The Sharks third baseman was pointing frantically at the bag and claiming that Kiyoshi hadn't touched it!

Coach Flaherty immediately stormed across the field to protest. That brought the Sharks coach out of his dugout and the umpires from their assigned spots. They began arguing loudly. Suddenly, Coach Flaherty jerked forward and knocked the Sharks coach in the head with the brim of his cap!

"That's it!" the head umpire shouted. "Yer out of here!"

Manny gasped in disbelief. Coach Flaherty had been ejected!

The coach couldn't seem to believe it, either. He started yelling at the umpire. But the umpire stood firm.

"Either you leave this park," he said in a loud ringing voice, "or we end this game now."

"But my team needs me!" Coach Flaherty protested.

"You should have thought of that before you brimmed him," the umpire retorted. "In the meantime, have your assistant coach take over for you."

To Manny's amazement, the coach looked embarrassed. "I don't have an assistant coach."

"Well, then," the umpire said, "I guess you'll have to forfeit. I can't let your squad play without a coach, and I'm not going to change my ruling."

Manny had been hoping for a quick end to the game. But not like this.

"Wait!" He grabbed his father's arm and started dragging him onto the field. "We do have an assistant coach! He's right here!"

Mr. Griffin opened his eyes wide. "Me?"

"Come on, Dad, please?" Manny begged. "You've come to every game, you know every player's strengths and weaknesses, and—and you just have to do it, that's all!"

His father gave him a long look and then smiled. "I suppose I could," he said. "But only if the umpire agrees."

"If he does," Manny said, "the first thing you have to do is to take Stu out of the game, okay?"

Mr. Griffin looked mystified by the request but didn't say anything. Instead, he joined the coaches and officials to discuss the matter of his coaching the game to its conclusion.

Now's my chance, Manny thought. He hurried over to the stands, where the spectators were buzzing with excitement over the ejection.

"Mrs. Fletcher!" he cried. "Mrs. Fletcher, can I talk to you? It's about Stu. Something happened to him that you need to know about."

When she was near, he blurted out the whole story—how the accident had happened, how he had come to realize that Stu was suffering from a concussion, and how today the team had worked so hard to keep Stu out of danger.

"But I know now that he wasn't out of danger, not really," he finished. "I'm sorry I didn't tell you sooner. And I would have, except I promised Stu I wouldn't."

Mrs. Fletcher stood very still. Then she

reached down and gave Manny a quick hug. "Thank you for telling me. I know it wasn't easy for you to break your promise to my son. Stu is lucky to have you for a friend."

Manny dug his toe into the dirt. "Too bad he won't want to be my friend anymore, not after he finds out I told you, and that I told my dad to take him out of the game," he said with a sigh. Then he looked up. "But I'd rather have him angry with me than knocked out at second."

18

Mrs. Fletcher didn't wait for Mr. Griffin to take Stu out of the game. She took him out herself. Manny learned later that she'd driven him straight to the doctor's office. There he received a definite diagnosis of a concussion and an order to stay off the field for the next month.

Meanwhile, Mr. Griffin was given permission to assume coaching duties for the remainder of the championship match. He did pretty well at it, too—the Grizzlies won, three runs to two. The score might have looked different if Sean, subbing in for

Stu at second, hadn't hit a double that sent Gary across home plate during the Grizzlies' last turn at bat.

But everyone agreed that Manny had the play of the game. It happened at the bottom of the sixth. The Sharks needed one run to send the game into extra innings. They had a chance to get that one and more, for although they had two outs, the bases were loaded.

The batter got the count to three and two. On the next pitch, he hit a short-arcing pop fly into foul territory just to the right of the plate. Manny yanked off his mask, dove sideways with his glove outstretched, and nabbed the ball just before it hit the ground.

With that catch, the Grizzlies were crowned the league champs! The players were presented with individual trophies, and Mr. Griffin was handed a large team trophy, which he accepted with a rather embarrassed shrug.

The Griffins and the rest of the parents decided to celebrate the victory by taking the team out for pizza and ice cream. While they were waiting for their food to arrive, Mr. Griffin excused himself to make a phone call. Manny was going to ask who he was talking to when the waiters delivered their pizza. Then all he cared about was getting a slice of the pie!

Manny was digging into his second slice of pepperoni when someone started tapping a glass with a fork. He looked up and almost choked with surprise. It was Coach Flaherty.

"Hello, boys, parents." He found Mr. Griffin and smiled. "Coach Griffin, thank you for filling in for me, and for calling to let me know you all were here. Now if you don't mind, I'd like to say a few words."

Manny nudged his father. "Is he going to start screaming again?"

Mr. Griffin smiled and shook his head.

Coach Flaherty cleared his throat. "I'm sure you all can hear me just fine. You know how I'm sure? Because I'm a LOUD-MOUTH! Know why I'm a loudmouth? Because I love the game of baseball so much, I just can't help myself sometimes!"

He grinned broadly and a few of the players snickered.

"I'm also a demanding coach," he continued. "So demanding, in fact, that I might just have rubbed some of you the wrong way." He met Manny's eyes and gave a small nod.

Then he shook his head. "I've just learned, too, that I was so caught up in wanting to win the championship that I ignored some very important signs. Those signs pointed to trouble for one of our players. You all know

I'm talking about Stu. When he started acting out of character, I should have realized that something was wrong. As his coach, I should have taken the time to find out what that something was."

Everyone was silent, thinking about what the coach had said. Then Mr. Griffin got to his feet and picked up the team trophy. "Coach Flaherty, on behalf of the Grizzlies, it's my pleasure to present this championship award to you. I think I speak for all of them when I say, job well done!"

The players broke out into hearty applause that only stopped when Coach Flaherty held up his hands for quiet. "Thank you, everyone, and especially to you, Mr. Griffin, for stepping into my shoes today. I hope it wasn't too much trouble?"

"Not at all," Manny's father said. "In fact, it was fun."

The coach grinned broadly "Glad to hear

it, because I could really use an assistant coach next season. What do you say?"

Manny's father straightened his glasses and grinned. "It would be my pleasure!"

Manny and his parents returned home that night full of pizza and ice cream. Up in his room, Manny tucked his trophy onto his bookshelf. He was changing into his sleep shirt and shorts when he heard the phone ring. His mother called up that it was for him.

"It's Stu," she said, handing him the receiver.

"Hey, Manny," Stu said.

"Hey back at you! How are you—oh, never mind. I already know what you're going to say. 'I'm fine,' right?"

Stu chuckled. "Yeah, that sounds like me. But guess what? Turns out I'm not fine after all. But you knew that, didn't you?"

"Yeah," Manny said quietly. "Listen, Stu, I'm sorry I ratted on you."

"No, I'm sorry I made you make that stupid promise. I'm sorry I went all berserk on you, too."

Manny smiled. "Yeah, it was like you were out of your head or something!"

"Very funny." Manny could hear the laughter in Stu's voice. "As it turns out, that's exactly what was happening. The doctor said irritability is sometimes a side effect of a concussion."

Neither of them said anything for a moment. Then Manny asked, "So, are we cool?"

"Cool? We're better than cool. We're teammates, man, champions! Oh, that reminds me: Sign up for summer baseball, okay? I may be out at second for now, but come July, I'll be back in action!"

Manny laughed. "I'll be there! You can count on me."

"Yeah," Stu said. "I know. See you tomorrow, Manny."

Manny hung up the phone. Then he grabbed his notebook of scorecards and hurried downstairs. "Hey, Coach, you got a minute for your favorite player or what?"

All available in paperback from Little, Brown and Company

**Previously published as Baseball Pals

Matt Christopher®

Muhammad Ali	Michael Jordan
Kobe Bryant	Peyton and Eli Manning
Dale Earnhardt Sr.	Shaquille O'Neal
Jeff Gordon	Albert Pujols
Tony Hawk	Jackie Robinson
Dwight Howard	Alex Rodriguez
LeBron James	Babe Ruth
Derek Jeter	Tiger Woods